2/96

CREATIVE EDUCATION

BUFFALO SABRES

JOHN GILBERT

Published by Creative Education
123 South Broad Street, Mankato, Minnesota 56001
Creative Education is an imprint of The Creative Company

Designed by Rita Marshall
Cover Illustration by Rob Day

Photos by: Bruce Bennett Studios, Focus on Sports, Hockey Hall of Fame,
Spectra Action and Wide World Photos

Library of Congress Cataloging-in-Publication Data

Gilbert, John, 1942-
Buffalo Sabres / John Gilbert.
p. cm. -- (NHL Today)
ISBN 0-88682-670-5

1. Buffalo Sabres (Hockey team)--History--Juvenile literature.
[1. Buffalo Sabres (Hockey team)--History. 2. Hockey--History.]
I. Title. II. Series.

GV848.B83G55   1995   93-47952
796.962'64'0974797--dc20

123456

Center Pat LaFontaine and right wing Alexander Mogilny race down the ice together. The clicking of crisp passes back and forth off their stick-blades resounds above the murmurs from the crowd at the Buffalo Memorial Auditorium, home of the Buffalo Sabres hockey team. As the two Sabres stars move in on the opponent's goal, the Buffalo fans sense that something special is about to happen on the ice. They slide to the edges of their seats in anticipation.

LaFontaine weaves past a final opposing defenseman, fakes a shot and sends the puck deceptively to the goalkeeper's left

Alexander Mogilny is one of the Sabres' top scorers.

side, where Mogilny directs it into the net for another Sabres score.

For Buffalo fans, a LaFontaine-Mogilny rush has become a common sight in the 1990s. But the fans never grow tired of watching these local heroes weave their magic on the ice as they help the Sabres return to their former position near the top of the National Hockey League standings.

Joe Daley set the all-time Sabres' record for most saves in a game with 64.

Since the team's debut during the 1970–71 season, the Buffalo Sabres have had many exciting hockey teams featuring gifted individual skaters and scorers. Besides LaFontaine and Mogilny, sharpshooters such as Gilbert Perreault, Rick Martin, Rene Robert, Dave Andreychuk, Danny Gare, Craig Ramsay, Mike Foligno and Dale Hawerchuk have all lit up the goal lights at "the Aud" time after time and brought Sabres fans to their feet cheering.

FLURRIES OF SNOW—AND GOALS

Buffalo is located on the western end of the state of New York, on the extreme eastern end of Lake Erie and just south of Lake Ontario. The second largest city in the state, it is far from the bustling metropolitan scene of New York City, both in miles and in lifestyle. Every summer, the Buffalo area draws thousands of tourists who visit Niagara Falls. But in the winter, Buffalo is more famous for its ferocious weather. Moisture builds up as fronts cross the eastern Great Lakes, and that moisture tends to be deposited as soon as it reaches land—which means in the Buffalo vicinity. In any given winter, snowfalls around Buffalo may approach or exceed 100 inches.

Because of its wintry environment and nearness to the Canadian border, Buffalo has long been a hotbed of amateur and professional hockey. Between the 1930s and 1960s, the city's pro fran-

Rookie Danny Gare scored 62 points in 1974-75 (page 7).

chise, the Bisons, was one of the top-ranking teams in minor league hockey, earning five Calder Cups as American League champs. Buffalo hockey fans loved their Bisons, but their dream was to cheer for a hometown National Hockey League club. That dream came true in 1970, when the NHL awarded expansion franchises to both Vancouver and Buffalo.

George "Punch" Imlach finished his first of two seasons coaching the Sabres.

Team owners decided to put an old hand in charge of the new club, naming George "Punch" Imlach as the Sabres' first coach and general manager. Just three years earlier, in 1967, Imlach had led the Maple Leafs in nearby Toronto, Ontario, to the Stanley Cup. Imlach's hiring brought instant credibility to the Buffalo club.

THE FRENCH CONNECTION

Most expansion teams suffer through several lean years before becoming successful, but Imlach immediately began building a high-scoring club to captivate Buffalo-area hockey fans. The key to the first Sabres squad was the team's first-ever draft choice, Gil Perreault. Perreault was a dashing, quick centerman with great scoring skills first displayed while playing junior hockey in Montreal. "You could start a franchise with him," Bernie Geoffrion once said. And that is what Buffalo did.

When Perreault stepped on the Aud ice for the first time in 1970, he was only 19 years old, but he played like a veteran. He scored 38 goals and added 38 assists during the 1970–71 season, the most ever by an NHL rookie up to that time, and his performance earned him the Calder Trophy as the league's top first-year player. He went on to set club records in games played, goals, assists and total points before hanging up his skates in 1986.

Perreault's NHL rookie goal-scoring record lasted only one year. The next season, another Sabres newcomer, Rick Martin, tallied 44 times at left wing to establish a new league mark.

One year later, in the 1972–73 season, Imlach added the final piece to a superior offensive line when he obtained right winger Rene Robert. Since Perreault, Martin and Robert were all of French-Canadian descent, they became known as "The French Connection," which also was the title of a popular movie in the early 1970s.

In hockey, much of a team's success depends on the ability of players to anticipate almost instinctively their teammates' moves on the ice. That is how strong lines develop a unified chemistry and perform well-coordinated plays. The French Connection certainly fit that pattern for success. All three men seemed to think alike, which helped them anticipate each other's plays and turned the Sabres into one of the NHL's highest-scoring squads.

Having developed a solid offensive punch, Sabres management turned to bolstering the team's defense as well. Rookie Jim Schoenfeld and veteran Tim Horton joined Buffalo for the 1972–73 season and provided excellent back-line support.

The three-year-old Sabres got off to a great start that season, moving well over the .500 mark. However, it took a win in the final game of the season for Buffalo to earn its first playoff berth.

Sabres fans were thrilled but nervous as they lined up for play-off tickets. Buffalo's initial opponent would be the legendary Montreal Canadiens, Stanley Cup winners in five of the previous eight years. Most fans were not surprised when Montreal won the first three games of the series, but they took notice when the Sabres won the next two. A record crowd of 15,668 packed the Aud for Game 6. In a tough battle, the Canadiens came out on top, 4-2, and eliminated Buffalo from the playoffs.

1 9 7 4

Rene Robert began one of his best seasons ever, finishing with 100 points.

Gil Perrault scored 81 game-winning goals for Buffalo (pages 10-11).

Jim Schoenfeld summed up the club's state of mind after the loss. "I feel like a loser," he said. "I'll feel that way for a couple of days and then I'll feel like a winner again. We have a lot of tomorrows ahead of us in this league."

A LOT OF PUNCH

The Sabres began the 1973–74 season with high hopes. However, injuries to key players disrupted the team's delicate chemistry and led to inconsistent performances. Then, in February 1974, the tragic death of Tim Horton in an automobile accident sent Buffalo players reeling. The club ended up in fifth place in its division and failed to reach the playoffs. To honor their late teammate, the Sabres established the Tim Horton Memorial Award, which is given each year to the player whose performance has far exceeded the recognition he has attained.

By the next season, everything began to click for the Sabres and Buffalo became one of the NHL's top teams. Despite having to face traditional NHL powers such as Boston and Montreal in the Adams Division, the Sabres won Adams Division titles in 1974–75, 1979–80 and 1980–81. After missing the playoffs in their first two years, they failed to qualify for the postseason tournament only three times in the next 21 years.

1 9 7 5

The Sabres renamed the Unsung Hero Award the Tim Horton Memorial Award in his memory.

The key to the club's success was the offensive attack that Punch Imlach had built around The French Connection. In 1974–75, the line was at its hottest. Martin set a club goal-scoring record with 52, while Robert and Perreault led the team in points (goals plus assists) with 100 and 96, respectively. And heading up a second line was high-scoring Danny Gare. They led the Sabres to the Adams Division title with a 49-16-15 record, the most wins and fewest losses in Buffalo's history.

The Sabres also went on to capture their first-ever playoff series in 1975, beating the Chicago Blackhawks four games to one in a best-of-seven opening-round series. Next came the powerful Canadiens, the club that had eliminated Buffalo two years earlier. The Sabres jumped ahead with a 6-5 victory when Gare scored in overtime and followed that success with a 4-2 triumph in the Aud. Even getting drubbed 7-0 and 8-2 in Montreal failed to blunt the Sabres, who came back home and won 5-4 in overtime when Robert connected. The Sabres returned to the Montreal Forum to wrap up the series with a 4-3 verdict in the sixth game.

In the Stanley Cup finals, Buffalo fell 4-1 and 2-1 in Philadelphia. When the series shifted to Buffalo, the Aud became famous for another NHL "first." Heat and high humidity outside caused a fog to rise from the chilly ice surface, and the games had to be stopped occasionally to let the fog clear.

Robert emerged from the fog to score another overtime winner for Buffalo's 5-4 victory in the third game, and the Sabres got even at two games apiece with a 4-2 victory in the fourth game. But the rugged Flyers shut down the Sabres offense after that, winning 5-1 in Philadelphia and capturing the Cup with Bernie Parent's shutout in a 2-0 sixth game in the Aud.

At the time, it seemed like only a temporary setback for a Sabres team poised to become one of the NHL's repeat visitors to the Stanley Cup finals. But they went into the mid-1990s without ever having attained that level again.

John Van Boxmeer began a two-season streak as the top scoring defenseman.

CHANGEOVER TO DEFENSE

During the next four seasons, the Sabres finished second in their division each year during the regular season. It was in the playoffs, however, that the team continually faltered. The club never was able to advance past the second round, despite the offensive mastery that Punch Imlach had developed for the club.

Before the 1979–80 season, Scotty Bowman replaced Imlach as general manager and also assumed the coaching reins temporarily. Bowman, who had led the Canadiens to five Stanley Cups in the 1970s, thought some changes were needed if the Sabres were to become Cup contenders. His philosophy was that scoring got headlines, while defense won championships and he started to alter the club's all-offense outlook.

Bowman closed down The French Connection when he sent Rene Robert to Colorado for defensive star John Van Boxmeer and Rick Martin to Los Angeles for a third-round draft choice. Martin, unfortunately, injured his knee badly enough to force retirement shortly after that. Later in 1981, Bowman shipped out Don

Jim Schoenfeld was one of the NHL's top defensemen (page 15).

Craig Ramsay had a shooting percentage of 21.8, the best on the team.

Luce, Danny Gare and Jim Schoenfeld in a blockbuster trade that brought Mike Foligno, Dale McCourt and Brent Peterson to the Sabres. The old gang was breaking up, but Bowman was intent on putting the Sabres over the top in his own way.

"I think sometimes the talent here is overrated because they've scored so much," Bowman noted. "There is a lot of good individual skill, but success in hockey comes down to self-discipline—knowing when to go to the net, or when to pick up a loose forward in our end."

Buffalo's top draft choices from the amateur ranks also reflected the team's new emphasis on defense, with such standouts as Larry Playfair, Mike Ramsey and Phil Housley joining the club in the late 1970s and early 1980s. By drafting Ramsey and Housley, Bowman took a gamble that paid off richly for the Sabres. Taking

Bob Sauve's goaltending helped boost the team's standings.   17

Keith Carney played tough defense for Buffalo.

As a rookie, Phil Housley scored 66 points, beginning a career as a top-scoring defenseman.

players from the Canadian junior ranks, with their long playing seasons, was the logical NHL practice. Yet both Ramsey and Housley were from high school programs in Minnesota, which played limited 20-game schedules. Ramsey had gone from Minneapolis Roosevelt High School to the University of Minnesota, where his team won the NCAA championship his freshman year. Then he left college at age 19 to play for the 1980 U.S. Olympic team, which won the gold medal at Lake Placid, and joined the Sabres before the end of the 1979–80 campaign.

He had a long and distinguished career in Buffalo, where he played at least part of 14 seasons until he was traded to Pittsburgh during 1992–93. Ramsey twice won the Memorial Trophy, presented to the team's most valuable player as voted by his teammates. He also received the Tim Horton Memorial Award two times as the team's most unsung hero.

Housley signed in 1982, right after finishing at South St. Paul High School. Joining the Sabres when he was 18, Housley played eight often-spectacular seasons before going to Winnipeg in the 1990 deal that brought Dale Hawerchuk to the Sabres. Housley was a special type of player and one of Bowman's favorites. He was a flashy defenseman so quick and clever that Bowman frequently used him as a center.

1 9 8 7

Mike Foligno led the team in goal-scoring for the second consecutive season.

A PLAYOFF JINX

The Sabres' playoff futilities continued—and even worsened—in the 1980s. In the 1981 playoffs, for example, the Sabres dispatched the Vancouver Canucks in the preliminary round in three straight games and were overwhelming favorites against the Minnesota North Stars in the next round, starting in the Aud. But the North Stars were leading a charmed life that carried them to the Cup finals that spring, and they whipped the Sabres in five games.

Following those frustrating 1981 playoffs, the Sabres would win only one preliminary-round playoff series over the next 12 years. They even failed to reach the postseason tournament in 1986 and 1987. Players, coaches and general managers came and went. Buffalo teams maintained solid records and outstanding scoring each regular season during this period but seemed to be jinxed when it came to playoff time.

In 1982, the Sabres lost three games to one against Boston in the opening playoff round. In 1984, they shocked Montreal with a three-game sweep in the preliminary round, riding Bob Sauve's hot goaltending to 1-0 and 3-0 victories in Montreal, and clinching the series 4-2 in Buffalo. (Sauve had four playoff shutouts

Ray Sheppard was an NHL Rookie of the Month in 1988.

in his Buffalo career—more than all other Sabres' goaltenders combined.) The momentum from the Montreal win carried over to a 7-4 victory over Boston to start the next round, but the Sabres ultimately lost a wrenching, double-overtime seventh game in Boston.

The first-round jinx resumed in 1984, when Quebec swept the Sabres in three straight; in 1985, when the Nordiques won a 6-5 deciding fifth game; in 1988, when Boston won four games to two; in 1989, when Buffalo blitzed Boston 6-0 in the opening game but then lost four in a row; in 1990, when Buffalo also won the opener but lost in six games against Montreal; and in 1991, when Montreal again beat the Sabres in six.

Pierre Turgeon led the Sabres in goals (34), assists (54) and points (88).

In 1992, the Sabres and Boston Bruins put on an exceptional seven-game series. The Sabres beat the Bruins 3-2 in Boston, then lost 3-2 in overtime. At the Aud, the Sabres fell 3-2. That string of three straight 3-2 scores was snapped when the Sabres lost 5-4 in overtime. Then they rallied to win 2-0 in Boston and 9-3 in Buffalo to tie the series at three games apiece. But the Bruins ultimately prevailed, 3-2, in the seventh game.

READY FOR THE 1990S

Forwards Dave Andreychuk, Mike Foligno and Pierre Turgeon, defensemen Phil Housely and Mike Ramsey and goaltender Tom Barrasso led the Sabres through the late 1980s. Ted Sator and former Sabres players Rick Dudley, Craig Ramsay and Jim Schoenfeld tried their hands at coaching and breaking the playoff jinx. Gerry Meehan replaced Bowman as general manager in 1987, and he brought in John Muckler in 1991 to try a new coaching approach.

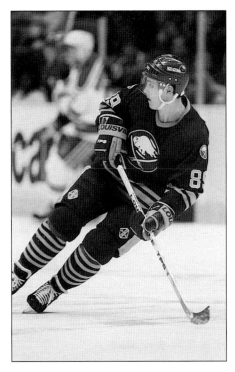

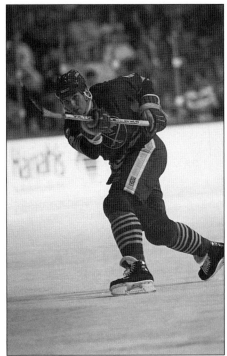

Left to right: Alexander Mogilny, Ken Sutton, Daren Puppa, Uwe Krupp.

When Muckler took over the coaching duties, two cornerstones of the "new" Sabres were already in place: Alexander Mogilny and Pat LaFontaine. Meehan had drafted Mogilny out of the Soviet Union's Elite League in 1988 and enticed him to defect a year later. In the Soviet Union, Mogilny played briefly for the Central Red Army team in Moscow, on a line with Sergei Fedorov at center and Pavel Bure on the other wing. Fedorov became an NHL star in Detroit and Bure a scoring sensation in Vancouver. All three are extremely fast, smart and creative players with the ability to score goals in large quantities. In Buffalo, Mogilny scored 15 goals as a 20-year-old in 1989–90 and increased it to 30 goals the next season, but that was just an indication of what was to come.

Donald Audette won the Fred T. Hunt Memorial Trophy as the Sabres' rookie of the year.

In 1991, Meehan sent Pierre Turgeon, Uwe Krupp and two other players to the New York Islanders to get LaFontaine, a star centerman who was born in St. Louis but had developed through youth hockey in Michigan and perfected his game in the high-intensity Quebec junior league.

LaFontaine was the leader of the 1984 U.S. Olympic team before entering the NHL, where he rose to professional stardom with the Islanders. His quick, darting style produced six consecutive seasons with more than 30 goals, including one 55-goal campaign and two 40-plus years.

In 1991–92, with both players in the Sabres lineup, Mogilny had 39 goals while LaFontaine totaled 46 goals, 47 assists and 93 points. But in 1992–93, the two scoring stars really exploded, with Mogilny breaking Rick Martin's team record for goals with 76 and LaFontaine amassing a club-record 148 points (53 goals and 95 assists), second highest in the league.

Center Pat LaFontaine had a stellar career in Buffalo (pages 26-27).

Despite Mogilny's and LaFontaine's heroics in 1992–93, Buffalo finished fourth in the Adams Division, behind Boston, Quebec and Montreal. After a decade of high finishes and disappointing playoffs, this time the Sabres reversed things. As fourth-place finisher, they were definite playoff underdogs going into Boston Garden to face the first-place Bruins.

Bob Sweeney scored in overtime for a 5-4 opening-game victory for Buffalo and goaltender Grant Fuhr shut out the Bruins for a 4-0 second-game upset. The series shifted to Buffalo and the Aud crowd saw Yuri Khmylev, another young Russian player, come through with the overtime winner for a 4-3 Buffalo victory. The fourth game was yet another shocker, as Buffalo completed an improbable four-game sweep with a 6-5 victory, again in overtime, this time with Brad May scoring.

The suddenly surging Sabres had to go to Montreal next. The Canadiens were destined to win the Stanley Cup, but it took four exciting games for them to conquer Buffalo. All four games were decided by identical 4-3 scores, the last three in overtime. Unfortunately for the Sabres, they lost both Mogilny and LaFontaine in the third game of the series, Mogilny with a broken ankle and LaFontaine with a twisted knee. It is impossible to project what a difference a healthy LaFontaine and Mogilny might have made to the Sabres' scoring attack. Still, the Sabres finally had broken through their playoff jinx for only the second time in 12 years.

LaFontaine's injured knee required major reconstructive surgery and he missed the entire 1993–94 season. Mogilny was still an imposing force, as was Dale Hawerchuk. In addition, the Sabres gained a promising newcomer when Derek Plante joined them

Grant Fuhr brought experience and expertise to the net.

Derek Plante scored 56 points in his rookie season.

as a rookie center instead of playing with the 1994 U.S. Olympic team. But without LaFontaine, the Sabres' chances at their first Stanley Cup were blunted.

Fortunately, LaFontaine fully recovered from his knee surgery. Now, with the dynamic duo of LaFontaine and Mogilny healthy and ready to lead the way, the Sabres stand poised as one of the NHL's most exciting teams of the 1990s.

1 9 9 5

Brad May continues to improve every year, adding points and shaving off penalty minutes.

Anaheim Mighty Ducks

Buffalo Sabres

Boston Bruins

Calgary Flames

Chicago Blackhawks

Dallas Stars

Detroit Red Wings

Edmonton Oilers

Florida Panthers

Hartford Whalers

Los Angeles Kings

Montreal Canadiens

New Jersey Devils

New York Islanders

New York Rangers

Ottawa Senators

Pittsburgh Penguins

Philadelphia Flyers

St. Louis Blues

San Jose Sharks

Tampa Bay Lightning

Toronto Maple Leafs

Vancouver Canucks

Washington Capitals

Winnipeg Jets